# AMAZING ANIMAL FACTS & LISTS

# AMAZING ANIMAL FACTS & LISTS

Sarah Khan

Edited by Phillip Clarke

Designed by
Luke Sargent and Adam Constantine

Digital imagery by Keith Furnival

Consultant: Dr Margaret Rostron

# Internet Links

Throughout this book, we have suggested interesting websites where you can find out more about the animal world. To visit the sites, go to the **Usborne Quicklinks** website at **www.usborne-quicklinks.com** and type the keywords "animal facts". There you will find links to click on to take you to all the sites. Here are some of the things you can do on the websites:

• become a dolphin-trainer

• become a wildlife photographer

• find your way through a virtual rainforest

• make your own animal

## Site availability

The links in **Usborne Quicklinks** are regularly reviewed and updated, but occasionally you may get a message that a site is unavailable. This might be temporary, so try again later, or even the next day. If any of the sites close down, we will, if possible, replace them with suitable alternatives, so you will always find an up-to-date list of sites in **Usborne Quicklinks**.

## Internet safety

When using the Internet, please make sure you follow these guidelines:

• Ask your parent's or guardian's permission before you connect to the Internet.

• If you write a message in a website guest book or on a website message board, do not include any personal information such as your full name, address or telephone number, and ask an adult before you give your email address.

• If a website asks you to log in or register by typing your name or email address, ask permission from an adult first.

• If you do receive an email from someone you don't know, tell an adult and do not reply to the email.

• Never arrange to meet anyone you have talked to on the Internet.

## Note for parents and guardians

The websites described in this book are regularly reviewed and the links in **Usborne Quicklinks** are updated. However, the content of a website may change at any time and Usborne Publishing is not responsible for the content on any website other than its own.

We recommend that children are supervised while on the Internet, that they do not use Internet Chat Rooms, and that you use Internet filtering software to block unsuitable material. Please ensure that your children read and follow the safety guidelines printed on the left. For more information, see the **Net Help** area on the **Usborne Quicklinks** website.

## Computer not essential

If you don't have access to the Internet, don't worry. This book is complete on its own.

# Contents

# Baby Animals

Many newborn animals are helpless and need a parent to feed and protect them. Mammals are the only animals that feed their babies with milk.

*This mother pig can feed eight babies at once from teats on her body.*

| Animal | Name of young |
|--------|---------------|
| Ape | Baby |
| Beaver | Kitten |
| Coyote | Whelp |
| Elephant | Calf |
| Goat | Kid |
| Gorilla | Infant |
| Hare | Leveret |
| Kangaroo | Joey |
| Llama | Cria |
| Platypus | Puggle |

**INTERNET LINK**

For a link to a website where you can watch a slide show of baby animal photographs, go to **www.usborne-quicklinks.com**

## Water birth

Baby dolphins and whales can only stay underwater for about 30 seconds at a time. They need to swim up to the surface to breathe. As soon as a baby is born, its mother pushes it to the surface so it can take its first breath.

*A baby whale is born tail first.*

*Its mother lifts it to the surface to breathe.*

## Growth spurt

A newborn polar bear cub is only the size of a guinea pig. It will grow to be as big as a car.

*This newborn polar bear is small enough to hide between its mother's toes.*

*At one year old, a polar bear cub is as big as a St. Bernard dog.*

## Pouch protection

A baby kangaroo is blind and so small that it could fit into a teaspoon. When a baby kangaroo is born, it crawls up into a pouch on its mother's stomach. It stays there for six months, until it is big enough to survive on its own.

*A newborn kangaroo crawls from its mother's birth opening, up her tummy and into a pouch.*

*Inside the pouch, the baby fastens onto a teat to suck milk.*

*This baby kangaroo is getting too big for its mother's pouch. It is around six months old.*

A female common vole can have babies when she is just 15 days old. She might have four to nine babies at a time, up to 15 times a year. In her lifetime, she may have 33 litters, giving birth to as many as 300 babies. This is more than any other mammal.

Some types of mouse opossum give birth to babies that are as small as grains of rice.

| Mammals with longest pregnancies | Average pregnancy |
|---|---|
| African elephant | 21 months |
| Asian elephant | 20 months |
| White rhinoceros | 16 months |
| Pilot whale | 16 months |
| Camel | 15 months |
| Black rhinoceros | 15 months |
| Giraffe | 14 months |
| Brazilian tapir | 13 months |
| Blue whale | 12 months |
| Sei whale | 12 months |
| African buffalo | 11 months |
| Walrus | 11 months |

## Holding on

A female opossum has 18 or so babies, and she keeps them all in one large pouch. After around ten weeks, the babies are too big for the pouch. Instead, they cling onto their mother's body anywhere they can – even onto her tail.

*Baby opossums cling onto their mother's body.*

# Growing Up

Although most newborn baby animals cannot look after themselves, some mature and become independent very quickly. Others need their mothers to look after them for a long time, protecting them from danger and teaching them how to find food.

## Mean males

Young male hippos face an unusual danger in the form of older male hippos, who can be very fierce when guarding their territory. Young males stay near their mothers for protection.

*This male hippo is not yawning, but showing off his sharp teeth to warn off rivals.*

Baby elephants are looked after by babysitters known as "aunties". When a mother elephant needs a break, another female from the herd looks after her baby. Sometimes aunties even produce milk to feed the baby. They will also care for the baby if the mother dies.

## Return to safety

A young kangaroo hides from danger in its mother's pouch.

*Sensing danger, a young kangaroo runs to its mother's pouch.*

*It jumps in head first so that its tail and back feet are sticking out.*

*It then twists around inside the pouch and pokes its head out.*

## Growing up fast

Young gorillas develop twice as quickly as human babies. They begin to crawl at around two months old, ride on their mother's back at four months, and walk at nine months. They stay with their mothers until they are five years old.

*This four-month-old gorilla is hitching a ride on its mother's back.*

| Animal | Age of maturity |
|---|---|
| Bushbaby | 8 months |
| Bat | 1-2 years |
| Kangaroo | 2-3 years |
| Hyena | 2-3 years |
| Lion | 3-4 years |
| Giraffe | 4-5 years |
| Rhinoceros | 5-8 years |
| Hippopotamus | 7-9 years |
| Gorilla | 7-10 years |
| Chimpanzee | 8-10 years |
| Elephant | 10-13 years |
| Dolphin | 10-16 years |

**INTERNET LINK**
For a link to a website where you can play dolphin games, go to
**www.usborne-quicklinks.com**

*Dolphin friendships often last their whole lives.*

## Playtime

Young animals like to play, just like young children. Playing lets them practice hunting and survival skills. Young lions learn to fight and catch prey by pouncing on their playmates and swatting at their tails.

*Young lions pretending to fight*

## Dolphin gang

A young dolphin stays with its mother for 3-6 years. When it leaves her, it joins a gang of other young dolphins. The gang stays together for years, spending most of the time playing together. They hardly ever mix with adults.

*Dolphins play by balancing things on their snouts...*

*... blowing bubbles at each other...*

*... and herding fish.*

Shrews have big families, and they need to make sure no one gets lost. When the mother goes out for food, the children follow, each holding onto the one in front.

# Life Goes On

Some animals live for only a matter of months, others live longer than humans. The length of time an animal lives is called its lifespan. The normal process of being born, growing up and breeding is called a life cycle.

Moles usually live for four years.

| Mammals with shortest lives | Natural lifespan |
|---|---|
| 1 Long-tailed shrew | 12-18 months |
| 2 Mole | 3-4 years |
| 3 Armadillo | 4 years |
| 4 European rabbit | up to 5 years |
| 5 European hedgehog | 6 years |

Many animals die before completing their life cycle. They might:

- run out of food and starve
- be caught and eaten by a predator
- die of a deadly disease

Will this Arctic hare live to a ripe old age?

## Sea life

Most sea animals, such as dolphins and whales, can live longer than most land animals. This may be because their bodies are cradled and supported by water and so are not worn out so quickly by the effects of gravity.

Dolphin

INTERNET LINK
For a link to a website about the life cycle of elephants, go to
**www.usborne-quicklinks.com**

| Mammals with longest lives | Natural lifespan |
|---|---|
| 1 Bowhead whale | 150-200 years |
| 2 Fin whale | 85-90 years |
| 3 Human | 75-80 years |
| 4 Asian elephant | 70-75 years |
| 5 Orca | 50-70 years |

Scientists can work out the age of some dolphins and whales by looking inside their ears. They have plugs in their ears, made from layers of keratin (the substance which makes up hair and nails). Each year, new layers grow, a little like rings on a tree trunk. Scientists count the layers to tell how old the animal is.

Ear plug rings

Position of ear plug

# Long captivity

Animals in captivity usually live longer than animals in the wild because their life is easier and they have no predators.

*Most shrews live fast and die young.*

The oldest known orang-utan lived in Philadelphia Zoo, USA, and died at the age of 57. Orang-utans usually live for 40-45 years in the wild.

45      57

The oldest known bat lived in London Zoo, England, and died at the age of 31. Bats usually live for 10-20 years in the wild.

20   31

The oldest known lion lived in Cologne Zoo, Germany, and died at the age of 29. Lions usually live for 12-14 years in the wild.

14   29

The oldest known tiger lived in Adelaide Zoo, Australia, and died at the age of 26. Tigers usually live for 10-15 years in the wild.

15   26

 *Usual lifespan in the wild (years)*

● *Longest lifespan in captivity (years)*

## Short life

Most shrews live for only 12-18 months in the wild. They are born one year, breed the next year and then die. The record lifespan for a shrew in captivity is two years and three months.

The oldest known elephant was a circus entertainer. During her career, Modoc, an Asian elephant, became a national heroine when she saved the circus lions from a terrible fire by dragging their cage out of a burning tent.

She starred in several American TV series before retiring to California, where she died in 1975, aged 75.

*Modoc the Asian elephant had a long and glittering career.*

## Living room

Lemmings' lives follow strange four-year patterns. For three years, they breed and their population grows. In the fourth year, overcrowding makes them leave home in their millions, searching for more space. Their journey may be long and difficult, and many die on the way. Some even try to cross rivers and seas, drowning in the attempt.

*Lemmings in search of more space*

# Animal Giants

Blue whales are the biggest animals that have ever lived. A female is around 30m long and can weigh as much as 190 tonnes – as heavy as 20 African elephants. Its tongue alone weighs three tonnes – heavier than 35 men. Its heart is as big as a car and its tail is as wide as the wings of an aeroplane.

*A blue whale can dive to depths of 500m below the surface of the ocean.*

## Largest on land

Male African elephants are the largest animals on land. They weigh 4-7 tonnes and are around 3.5m tall at the shoulder – twice as tall as an average-sized person.

Kell, a Mastiff dog living in Leicestershire in England, is as heavy as a baby elephant. In 1999, the dog weighed 130kg. He is fed on a diet that contains lots of protein such as beef, eggs, and goat's milk.

*A male African elephant weighs as much as three family cars.*

## Skyscrapers

With their long necks and legs, giraffes are the tallest animals. An adult Masai giraffe can be over 5m tall. A tall person only comes up to the top of its leg.

*A Masai giraffe is three times as tall as this Masai warrior.*

## Heavy jumper

Red kangaroos can grow up to 1.8m tall and weigh up to 90kg – as much as a heavyweight boxer. Their metre-long tails balance the weight of their bodies when they jump. They are the biggest of all pouched mammals, or marsupials.

| Animal group | Biggest species | Average weight |
|---|---|---|
| Mammal | Blue whale | 130 tonnes |
| Horse | Belgian stallion | 1.5 tonnes |
| Bear | Polar bear | 1 tonne |
| Antelope | Giant eland | 898kg |
| Deer | Alaskan moose | 816kg |
| Cat | Siberian tiger | 250kg |
| Ape | Mountain gorilla | 180kg |

## Big appetite

Siberian tigers are the largest members of the cat family. They can grow to 3m from nose to tail and can weigh up to 300kg. They can eat as much as 45kg of meat in one night – enough to make 400 hamburgers.

*A Siberian tiger can drag prey in its jaws that would be too heavy for six men.*

## INTERNET LINK

For a link to a website where you can find the biggest animals and other animal record-breakers, go to **www.usborne-quicklinks.com**

## Brain box

Sperm whales have the heaviest brains. Their brains weigh up to 9kg – six times heavier than a human brain. The whale has a very large head which is around one third of its body length, so there is plenty of room for its huge brain.

*Sperm whales are the world's largest meat-eating animals.*

The biggest seal ever recorded was an elephant seal that was over 6.5m long and, with its head up, was 3m tall – almost twice the height of an average-sized man.

13

# Small Animals

Savi's pygmy shrews are the world's smallest mammals. They are so small that they can look for food in tunnels made by earthworms.

*Savi's pygmy shrew – the size of a finger.*

The smallest dog ever known was a Yorkshire terrier the size of a hamster. It measured 6.3cm tall at the shoulder, only 9.5cm from nose to tail and it weighed just 113g.

## Heartbeats

The smaller an animal is, the faster its heart beats. This is because smaller animals are more active than larger ones.

| Animal | Average heart rate (beats per minute) |
|--------|---------------------------------------|
| Horse  | 50  |
| Cow    | 60  |
| Human  | 70  |
| Rabbit | 200 |
| Bat    | 300 |
| Mouse  | 600 |
| Shrew  | 800 |

## INTERNET LINK

For a link to a website where you can visit a virtual small mammal house, go to **www.usborne-quicklinks.com**

| Animal group | Smallest species | Average weight (adult male) |
|--------------|------------------|-----------------------------|
| Squirrel | African pygmy squirrel | 10g   |
| Monkey   | Pygmy marmoset         | 120g  |
| Rabbit   | Pygmy rabbit           | 400g  |
| Cat      | Rusty-spotted cat      | 1.4kg |
| Fox      | Fennec fox             | 1.5kg |
| Antelope | Royal antelope         | 1.5kg |
| Deer     | Southern pudu          | 7kg   |
| Bear     | Sun bear               | 27kg  |
| Dolphin  | Commerson's dolphin    | 30kg  |
| Seal     | Ringed seal            | 60kg  |

The smallest horse in the world is Black Beauty, a miniature black mare the size of a cat. It is 47cm tall and weighs 19kg.

## Royal spoonful

Royal antelopes (the smallest antelopes in the world) have legs as thin as pencils. One living in London Zoo in England had hoofs so tiny that it was able to fit all four in a tablespoon.

# Tiny tramplers

Southern pudus (the world's smallest deer) eat bamboo leaves, but are so small that they can only get to the leaves by first trampling on the bamboo stalks. This flattens the plant and brings the leaves within reach.

Southern pudu

# Little record breakers

The silhouettes below show record-breaking animals at their actual size. They are shown in silhouette so you can easily compare their sizes.

**Smallest marsupial**
Long-tailed planigale:
9cm long,
weighs 4g

**Smallest mammal**
Savi's pygmy shrew:
6.5cm long,
weighs 2g

**Smallest flying mammal**
Bumblebee bat:
15cm wingspan,
weighs 1.9g

**Smallest meat-eating mammal**
Least weasel:
19cm long,
weighs 30g

# What's For Dinner?

Animals need a lot of energy for hunting, finding homes and looking after their young. They get their energy from food.

| Animal | How much it can eat in one day |
|---|---|
| Blue whale | 5 tonnes of krill |
| Sperm whale | 1 tonne of squid, fish and shrimp |
| African elephant | 227kg of leaves |
| Polar bear | 100kg of seal and fish |
| Hippopotamus | 45kg of fruit and grass |
| Bengal tiger | 45kg of red meat |
| Lion | 36kg of red meat |
| Camel | 32kg of fruit, leaves and grass |
| Giant panda | 30kg of bamboo shoots |
| Bottlenose dolphin | 15kg of fish |
| Brown bear | 15kg of roots, leaves and red meat |

*Coming to get you... actually, vampire bats don't attack people.*

## Liquid diet

A great vampire bat drinks around 70% of its body weight in blood every night. Vampire bats attack sleeping animals. Their saliva contains a substance that stops the prey's blood from clotting and closing the wound while the bat feeds.

*Koala*

## Low energy diet

A koala's diet doesn't give it much energy. It eats 600-800g of eucalyptus leaves each day. That is the same as a human surviving on just one bowl of cereal every day.

A Savi's pygmy shrew can't live for more than two hours without food and can eat up to three times its own weight in a day. A human would have to eat a sheep, 50 chickens, 60 loaves of bread and over 150 apples in one day to match the shrew's meals.

**INTERNET LINK**
For a link to a website where you can see whales catch their food, go to **www.usborne-quicklinks.com**

## Gone fishing

Brown bears in Alaska, North America, fish for salmon that swim up mountain rivers to breed. They catch the fish in different ways.

When a sea otter gets hungry in the water, it turns over onto its back, balances a large stone on its chest and opens clam shells by smashing them against the stone.

*Sea otter having a smashing time*

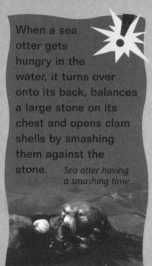

## Blowing bubbles

Humpback whales sometimes make bubble "nets" to catch food.

*The whale swims in an upward spiral, blowing air out of its blowhole to make bubbles.*

*They might snap up the fish in their powerful jaws...*

## Scavenger hunt

Meat eaters don't always kill their own food. Sometimes they feed on animals that have been killed by other animals or have died naturally. This is called scavenging. Many predators, such as lions and wild dogs, often scavenge.

*The bubbles rise to the surface, forcing up the small fish and krill trapped within the spiral.*

*...use their paws to flip the fish out of the water...*

*With its mouth open, the whale bursts out of the water and takes a huge gulp of food.*

*...or pin the fish to the river bed with their paws then grab them with their teeth.*

*A scavenging hyena has found part of a zebra for dinner.*

# How Animals Eat

Not many animals have hands, so they use other parts of their bodies to reach and grab their food.

## Reaching up

Giraffes have the longest necks in the animal kingdom, measuring up to 1.8m. Because they have such long legs as well, they can reach leaves on the highest branches. They use their 50cm long tongues to grip and pull branches down. Then they strip off the leaves with their rubbery lips.

A giant anteater has a 60cm tongue. It tears open anthills and termite mounds with its claws and then pokes its long, sticky tongue inside, coating it with insects. It can flick its tongue in and out twice a second and can catch over 30,000 insects a day.

*A giraffe's tongue is so tough that it can even grip thorns without getting hurt.*

## Terrific teeth

Animals have different types of teeth, depending on what food they eat.

**Canines** are dagger-like teeth that are used for piercing and killing prey.

*Hyena*

*Canine*

**Carnassials** are large, jagged teeth used for slicing meat.

*Lioness*

*Carnassial*

**Incisors** are small, front teeth that are used for biting and gnawing meat or plants.

*Horse*

*Incisors*

**Molars** are square teeth set inside an animal's cheek that are used for grinding plants.

*Chimpanzee*

*Molars*

## Taking the strain

Instead of teeth, some whales have stiff fringes, called baleen, hanging down inside their mouths. They use the baleen like a strainer, to strain food from water. Baleen is made of keratin, a substance found in your fingernails and hair.

*A whale opens its mouth and takes a huge gulp of water. The water is full of krill (small, shrimp-like creatures).*

*When it closes its mouth, the water is strained out through the baleen. The krill stays behind, trapped in the fringes.*

Hyenas have such strong jaws and stomachs that they can chew up and digest the skin, bones, horns and even the teeth of their prey.

## Strange stomachs

Cows have not one, but four stomach-like chambers in their bodies. After they have chewed and swallowed their food, it passes through two chambers, then comes back up to the mouth to be chewed again. Then it is swallowed for a second time and passes through the other two chambers. It is slowly digested along the way.

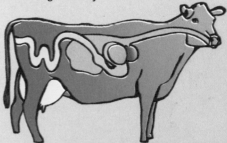

*The four different colours show the four chambers inside a cow's body.*

### INTERNET LINK

For a link to a website about the different ways animals eat, go to **www.usborne-quicklinks.com**

## Nosing around

Some animals use their noses not only to smell food, but to reach it as well.

African elephants use the two finger-like parts on the tips of their trunks to pick berries from the ground or pluck leaves from trees.

Echidnas poke their long, tough snouts into logs and termite mounds when searching for food.

Walruses drag themselves along the sea bed, using their muzzles to root out molluscs, worms and shrimps.

*Noses can be used for grasping...*

*...poking...*

*...or digging.*

# Super Senses

Animals have five main senses:

Touch

Sight

Hearing

Smell

Taste

Animals use their senses to collect information about their surroundings. Senses help them to find food, find a mate and avoid danger.

## Ear for echoes

Bats and dolphins are the mammals with the most sensitive hearing. They can tell where objects are, and how big they are, by giving out high-pitched sounds. The sound waves bounce off the objects and return to the animal. This is called echo location.

*A bat gives out a series of short, high-pitched sounds (shown in yellow).*

*The sounds bounce off nearby objects and return to the bat (returning sounds shown in blue).*

A bloodhound's nose is a million times more sensitive than a human's. It can follow a scent that is four days old.

*Bloodhounds help the police to track down criminals by following their scent.*

## Bright eyes

Cats are brilliant at seeing in the dark. They have a layer at the back of their eyes which acts like a mirror, reflecting and focusing light onto light sensor cells in their eyes.

*In bright light, the dark hole, or pupil, in the cat's eye is narrow, letting in only a little light.*

*In dim light, the pupil is wide, letting in any available light, which is then reflected.*

## Feeling around

A cat's whiskers stick out from its cheeks, chin and forehead and help it to feel its way around in the dark. Whiskers are so sensitive that they can pick up a change in the weather or even a movement in the air.

## Varying vision

Plant eaters need to see to the side as well as the front so they can keep a look out for predators while they graze. Most have eyes at the sides of their heads.

*Deer – eyes at the side*

**INTERNET LINK**
For a link to a website about amazing animal senses, go to **www.usborne-quicklinks.com**

A rabbit's tongue contains almost twice as many taste buds as a human's. Rabbits have around 17,000 taste buds while humans only have around 9,000.

Animals that hunt need to be able to focus clearly on the prey ahead of them as they give chase. Animals that live in trees need to be able to judge distances as they move from branch to branch. Both groups of animals have eyes at the front of their heads.

*Lion – eyes in front*

## Best beak

When underwater, a platypus shuts its eyes, ears and nostrils. It relies only on its sensitive beak to help it find food. The beak picks up tiny pulses of electricity given out by its prey.

*A platypus' beak is really a long snout covered with soft, leathery skin.*

| Eyes at the side (plant eaters) | Eyes at the front (hunters and tree-dwellers) |
| --- | --- |
| Cows | Apes |
| Deer | Bears |
| Giraffes | Cats |
| Mice | Dogs |
| Rabbits | Lions |
| Rats | Monkeys |
| Shrews | Raccoons |

## Nosy moles

A star-nosed mole spends most of its life underground feeling for food with the tentacles on its nose. These tentacles are almost six times more sensitive than your hand.

*The pink tentacles on the mole's nose feel around for food.*

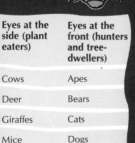

# Night Life

More types of mammal are active at night than during the day. These are called nocturnal mammals. There are several reasons why they prefer the night.

Foxes hunt at night because there are fewer other types of animal, such as birds of prey, looking for similar food.

Desert rats only go out at night, when the hot desert has cooled down.

Armadillos find it easier to hide from predators in the dark.

| Nocturnal animal | Habitat |
| --- | --- |
| Armadillo | Forests and plains of North and South America |
| Bushbaby | African forests |
| Duck-billed platypus | Streams and rivers of East Australia |
| Gerbil | African and Asian deserts |
| Giant panda | Mountain forests of China |
| Hippopotamus | Lakes and rivers of East Africa |
| Lion | African grasslands |
| Northern fur seal | Northern Pacific Ocean |
| Raccoon | Deciduous forests of North America |
| Red fox | Forests and deserts of Europe, America, Africa and Asia |
| Rhinoceros | African grasslands |
| Sloth | Rainforests of South and Central America |

## Ear plugs

Bushbabies have sharp hearing to help them find food at night. During the day, they have to sleep with their ears folded inwards to block out the noises of the forest.

Bushbabies get their name from the noises they make at night, which sound like the cries of a newborn baby.

*Bushbabies have huge eyes, but they rely more on hearing and smell.*

INTERNET LINK
For a link to a website about animal night vision, go to
**www.usborne-quicklinks.com**

# Hanging around

Flying foxes are really a type of bat. At night, they fly up to 65km in search of food. They spend their days hanging sleepily from trees, sometimes in extremely large groups called camps. On very hot days, they keep cool by fanning themselves with their wings.

*At night, flying foxes look for fruit and nectar to eat.*

*Flying foxes can hang from a branch by one foot, but cannot stand upright because their legs are not strong enough.*

# Shy devil

Tasmanian devils can look and sound very fierce, but they are really quite shy. During the day, they usually hide in dense forests. At night, they roam long distances – up to 16km – in search of food.

*This Tasmanian devil looks scary, but it is only making this face because it is frightened.*

# Night monkeys

Douroucoulis are the only nocturnal monkeys. They are sometimes called "owl monkeys" because of their huge eyes and the markings on their faces. They have very thick fur to keep them warm during cold nights.

Pygmy tarsiers are around 12cm long and their eyes are 1.5cm in diameter. That would be the same as a human having eyes the size of grapefruits.

Tarsiers need such big eyes to help them see in the dark.

*Tarsiers' eyes do not move but their heads can turn nearly 360°.*

*Douroucoulis have large eyes to help them see in the dark.*

23

# Tops and Tails

Many animals use their heads as weapons or to send messages. Some have antlers or horns to help them do this.

Other animals use their tails to send messages. Tails can also help them to hold onto objects, or to move quickly.

*A dolphin moves its tail up and down to help it move through the water.*

## Amazing antlers

Wapiti have the longest antlers. Their antlers can grow up to 1.8m wide (about the same length as a giraffe's neck) and weigh as much as 18kg (about as heavy as a three year old child).

*A wapiti's antlers will grow around 2.5cm each day until they reach their full length in summer.*

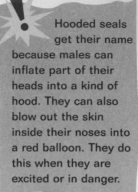

Hooded seals get their name because males can inflate part of their heads into a kind of hood. They can also blow out the skin inside their noses into a red balloon. They do this when they are excited or in danger.

*A hooded seal inflates its nose to twice the size of a football.*

*It can also blow the inside of its nostril out like a red balloon.*

## Wide load

The longest horns belong to the Indian water buffalo. A huge male, shot in 1955, had horns which measured 4.2m long from tip to tip – about twice as long as an elephant's trunk. Tame buffaloes usually have their horns trimmed.

*A water buffalo's thick horns curve inwards and backwards.*

## Long horn

The white rhinoceros has two horns. The front horn can grow up to 1.6m long, which is about three times as long as a human arm. If the horn breaks off it will grow back at a rate of about 5mm a month.

*The word rhinoceros actually means "nose horn".*

# Spider support

Spider monkeys have such strong tails that they can support their whole body weight with their tails alone.

## INTERNET LINK

For a link to a website about tops, tails and other body parts, go to **www.usborne-quicklinks.com**

## Long swatters

Asian elephants have the longest tails of all land mammals. They can grow up to 1.5m long – nearly as long as their trunks. Elephants use their tails as fly-swats.

A spider monkey uses its long tail as an extra limb as it moves from branch to branch.

| Land mammals with the longest tails | Tail length |
| --- | --- |
| Asian elephant | 1.5m |
| Leopard | 1.4m |
| African elephant | 1.3m |
| African buffalo | 1.1m |
| Giraffe | 1.1m |
| Red kangaroo | 1m |

## Balancing act

When a kangaroo hops quickly it uses its tail for balance. When it hops slowly it uses its tail to push its hind legs off the ground, as though it was a fifth leg.

A red kangaroo stretches its tail out as it hops quickly.

The ground squirrel of the Kalahari Desert in South Africa keeps cool by angling its tail over its head like a parasol.

A ground squirrel on the move makes its own shade.

## Tall tails

When ring-tailed lemurs are walking along the ground in search of food, each keeps its striped tail raised high in the air. This shows the others where they are and keeps the group safely together.

A dominant male lemur will walk with its head and tail held high.

25

# Coats and Camouflage

Hair on an animal has a lot of uses:

 It keeps an animal warm.

 It can make it look bigger.

 It can help it to hide.

 It can protect it from injury.

**!** Sloths move around so little that algae on the trees they hang from also begins to grow on their coats. The green algae helps to hide the sloth among the leaves.

*Unlike any other mammal, a sloth's hair grows from its stomach down towards its back.*

## Taking a stand

A hyrax has a useful patch of hair on its back. The hairs are longer and a different colour to the rest of its coat. When the hyrax is threatened, the hairs stand on end to make it look bigger and more scary.

*A happy hyrax*    *A scared hyrax*

## Warm coat

Arctic musk oxen have the longest fur. In winter, their outer layer of hair can grow up to 2m long. They also have a fleece undercoat. This helps them to survive in freezing temperatures as low as -60°C.

*Without its warm, double-layered coat, a musk ox would freeze to death during winter.*

## Marvellous mane

Young cheetahs have a thick mane of grey hair on their backs. The mane is about 8cm long and helps hide the cub among dry grasses and bushes. It also makes the cub look bigger and fiercer than it really is so it can scare away enemies.

*By the time it is two years old, this cheetah's mane will have disappeared.*

**INTERNET LINK**
For a link to a website about animal camouflage, go to
**www.usborne-quicklinks.com**

## All a blur

Zebras' striped coats look blurred in the hazy heat of the African grasslands. This makes the zebra's outline harder to see from a distance.

*It's hard to see where one zebra ends and the next begins...*

## Crouch for cover

When saiga antelopes sense danger, they crouch down and keep very still. Predators often mistake them for mounds of earth.

*From a distance, this crouching antelope would be hard to spot.*

Pangolins are the only mammals to have scales. The scales, like hedgehog quills, are made from hairs tightly joined together. Ordinary hairs grow between the scales and on the underside of a pangolin's body.

*A pangolin raises its sharp-edged scales when it's under attack.*

## Seasonal changes

Arctic hares, foxes and stoats change their coats twice a year. They have white coats in winter so they don't stand out against the snow. In summer, their coats are brown or grey to blend in with rocks and earth.

*An Arctic fox in summer...*

*...looks different from an Arctic fox in winter.*

## Blending in

Most big cats have yellow or brown fur with spotted or striped markings. At night or in patchy daylight this helps them to blend in with the light and shade of their surroundings.

*This leopard has dark spots on its coat that blend in with the dappled light of the rainforest.*

# Fight and Flight

Most animals in the wild are always in danger of being eaten. Some have clever and unusual ways of defending themselves or escaping from predators.

## Pin cushion

Porcupine quills can cause serious wounds. If attacked, a porcupine charges backwards, sticking quills into its attacker. As it moves away the quills are left behind.

*This dog has a face full of quills. It made the mistake of attacking a porcupine.*

A Canadian porcupine has about 30,000 quills, each up to 12cm long. Put end to end, they would reach a third of the way up Mount Everest.

## Facing the enemy

If an enemy threatens, male musk oxen stand shoulder to shoulder. They line up in front of their calves and females, with their horns facing the attacker. A male ox steps out to do battle. If he falls, others follow one by one until the predator leaves or is killed.

*Musk oxen form a wall-like defence.*

## Poison pals

Some animals use poison to kill or injure their attackers:

*Platypus*

Male duck-billed platypuses have poisoned spikes on their ankles, which they use to kick predators.

*Poisonous shrew*

Some types of shrew have poisons in their saliva. Shrew bites can paralyse small animals and cause painful skin swellings in people.

*Solenodon*

Solenodons are rare, shrew-like animals that live in Haiti and Cuba. Poison, strong enough to kill small animals, runs along grooves in their teeth.

Wood mice have disposable tails. If a mouse is grabbed by its tail, it sheds the skin that covers it. The bare tail that is left eventually shrivels and falls off.

*This cat got less than he bargained for.*

*Hold your nose...*

## Secret weapon

A skunk's tail hides a very effective weapon. When threatened, the skunk lifts its tail and squirts out a horrible-smelling liquid from a gland beneath it. The terrible stink can be smelt up to 500m away.

INTERNET LINK

For a link to a website where you can learn about animal defences, go to www.usborne-quicklinks.com

## Playing dead

The opossum fools its predators by pretending to be dead. When attacked, it rolls over and lies still, mouth open and eyes glazed over. The predator may then lose interest and go away.

No one knows if the opossum is playing dead or is simply paralysed with fear. After lying still for up to four hours, it looks around and, if the danger is over, comes back to life.

*Faking death, or scared stiff?*

## Warning signs

Some animals have warning signals that let other animals know about danger. They might also confuse or frighten a predator so that it does not attack.

*You'll never catch me...*

Springboks leap straight up into the air with arched backs. This is called pronking. It warns predators not to bother attacking such athletic creatures.

*Get ready to fight, or run...*

Horses snort, raise their tails and prick up their ears to alert other horses to danger.

*Listen to me!*

Hyraxes make loud screaming warning calls.

# Sending Messages

Animals have different ways to warn others of danger, mark their territory, call their young or find a mate – but most of them do it. They use smell, sight, sound and touch.

Hyenas "laugh" when afraid or excited.

## Laughing hyenas

Hyenas don't really have a sense of humour. Only human beings can really laugh. But hyenas hunt in teams and use different noises to communicate. They growl, grunt, whine and yelp but also burst into noisy choruses that can sound like hysterical laughter.

**!** A male orang-utan "burps" to keep other males out of his territory. He fills his throat pouch with air, swelling his face, and lets out a long call, ending with sighs – and bubbling burps.

## Sea songs

*Dolphins whistle to say hello.*

Dolphins have a wide vocabulary of over 32 sounds. They use squeals, clicks, barks and whistles to keep in touch with each other.

Whales build up a series of sounds into songs. A song may last for up to thirty minutes. Whales have very loud voices – some are even louder then jet planes.

*Humpback whales sing head down and tail up.*

| Loudest mammals | Sound level |
| --- | --- |
| Blue whale | 188 decibels |
| Hippopotamus | 115 decibels |
| Lion | 114 decibels |
| Elephant | 105 decibels |
| Bat | 100 decibels |
| Howler monkey | 90 decibels |
| Human (shouting) | 70 decibels |
| Dog | 50 decibels |

Howler monkeys "sing" loudly to warn off predators.

## Tail talk

Cats and dogs use their tails to show their feelings. A happy dog wags its tail, but if it's frightened, it puts its tail between its legs. An angry cat swishes its tail from side to side, but if it's happy, it holds its tail up in the air.

*A happy cat*    *A happy dog*

When two prairie dogs meet they "kiss" to find out if they know each other. If they don't, the intruder is driven away. If they do, they kiss again and start to groom each other.

*Prairie dogs will stop to kiss even when rushing away from danger.*

## Speaking scents

Tenrecs are small, hedgehog-like creatures from Madagascar. They mark their territory with their body smell. They spit where they want to mark, rub their paws along their sides to pick up their smell, and then rub their paws in the spit.

Ring-tailed lemurs rub their bottoms on trees as they travel through the forest. They leave their scent to mark their trails so that the rest of the troop know where the lemur has been.

*Tenrecs use saliva to mark their territory.*

*Ring-tailed lemurs leave a scent trail.*

---

### INTERNET LINK

For a link to a website where you can listen to a variety of animal noises, go to **www.usborne-quicklinks.com**

---

## Making faces

Chimpanzees are among the very few animals that can make faces to show their feelings. They can show anger, happiness and interest very much like human beings. But if a chimp seems to be grinning by showing its teeth, it's probably not smiling but expressing fear.

*This chimpanzee is making a "play face" – the expression it uses when it's playing, to show that it's happy.*

*This chimpanzee is unhappy.*

*This chimpanzee is afraid.*

# Animal Instincts

All animals have instincts – they automatically know how to do certain things to survive. Their instincts tell them how to find food, cope with extreme temperatures, breed and raise their young.

## Shifting seasons

During the dry season, grassland zebras migrate to the hills and forests where there is more rain.

*Zebras travel from grasslands to hills and back again.*

In winter, prairie bison migrate to valleys and woods where they find shelter from the cold.

*Bison travel from prairies to valleys and back again.*

## Migration marathons

Scientists think that some animals must have a sort of built-in compass. This is because they are able to migrate long distances, using the same routes every year without getting lost. They make these journeys to reach places where they can feed or breed.

| Longest migrators | Distance travelled (there and back) | Colour |
|---|---|---|
| Grey whale | 19,300km | ⇨ |
| Humpback whale | 13,000km | ⇨ |
| Northern fur seal (male) | 10,000km | ⇨ |
| Caribou | 4,600km | ⇨ |
| Noctule bat | 4,500km | ⇨ |
| European pipistrelle | 3,800km | ⇨ |

*The longest mammal migrations are made by sea.*

When grey whales migrate in winter, they make a 9,650km journey – about the same distance as from London to Tokyo. Starting from their feeding grounds in the Bering Straits, they travel south along the west coast of the USA to Mexico. The journey takes around 90 days. In the spring, they return north by the same route.

# Fast asleep

Instinct tells some animals to sleep through the times of the year when food is scarce. While they sleep, their body temperature drops and their pulse and breathing rate slows.

## Hibernation
Animals sleep through the cold winter months.

*Hibernating bear*

| Longest hibernators | Months spent hibernating |
|---|---|
| Barrow ground squirrel | 9 |
| Marmot | 7-8 |
| Black bear | 7 |
| Hamster | 6-7 |
| European hedgehog | 6 |

## Aestivation
Animals sleep through the hot summer months.

*Aestivating squirrel*

| Longest aestivators | Months spent aestivating |
|---|---|
| Uinta ground squirrel | 9 |
| Mojave ground squirrel | 7 |
| Yellow-bellied marmot | 4 |
| Desert jerboas | 3 |
| Cactus mouse | 3 |

INTERNET LINK
For a link to a website about black bears in hibernation, go to www.usborne-quicklinks.com

During hibernation, a marmot's body temperature drops to 10°C – low enough to kill a non-hibernating animal.

# Useful instincts

Some animals' instincts can be very useful to people:

Dolphins instinctively find and pick up objects underwater. Navies use dolphins to help retrieve tools lost at sea.

Dogs instinctively chase and round up prey. Shepherds use dogs to help them herd sheep.

*A single dog can control a large herd of sheep.*

Pigs instinctively sniff out food. Farmers use pigs to help them find truffles (a type of mushroom).

*The farmer has to grab the truffle quickly before the pig eats it.*

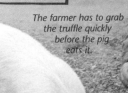

# Families and Herds

Many animals find it useful to live in groups. They can share food, look after each others' babies and groom each other. Groups of animals may hunt together so they can catch bigger prey. In larger groups, members may come and go. In smaller groups, they may stay together for longer, like a family.

The largest herd ever recorded was a group of over ten million springbok seen in southern Africa. The herd is said to have covered 5,360km$^2$ – over three times the area of London, England.

*Springbok roam African grasslands.*

## Group names

Some animal groups have very unusual names:

A clowder of cats
A leap of leopards
A pride of lions
A skulk of foxes
A labour of moles
A crash of rhinoceroses
A trip of goats
A shrewdness of apes

*These lionesses are all members of the same group, called a pride.*

## Standing tall

While a family of meerkats feed or doze, one member of the group will watch out for danger. It stands on its hind legs to see over the long grass.

*Alerted to danger, a meerkat family stands up to see what is approaching.*

## Elephant funerals

When an elephant dies, the herd mourns and stays by the body for several days. They cover it with leaves and earth before they move on.

| Animal | Approximate number in herd |
|---|---|
| Caribou | 500,000-750,000 |
| Bison | 2,000-4,000 |
| Springbok | 1,000-3,000 |
| Wapiti | 300-400 |
| Elephant | 150-250 |
| Wild horses | 10-20 |
| Zebra | 5-20 |

During the summer, Bracken Cave in Texas, USA, is home to as many as 20 million Mexican free-tailed bats.

*Naked mole rats huddle together to keep warm.*

## Sea support

If a sperm whale is injured, the other members of its group make a circle around it, supporting it near the surface so it can breathe.

*An injured sperm whale is supported in what is called a "marguerite" formation, named after a type of daisy.*

## Rat palace

Naked mole rats live in colonies of up to 300. In each colony, only one female has all the babies. She is the "queen" and is guarded by a couple of male "soldier" rats.

The rest of the colony are workers. They live and work as a group, digging tunnels in chain-gangs and sleeping huddled together.

*Mole rats work in a chain-gang, each one passing the freshly dug sand to the one behind.*

## Pack order

Wolves live in groups, called packs, of up to 20 members. Each wolf has its place in the pack's order of importance. You can tell how important a wolf is by the body language it shows to others in the pack.

Most important in pack

Second in importance in pack

Ordinary pack member

Least important in pack

INTERNET LINK
For a link to a website where you can meet the members of a wolf pack, go to **www.usborne-quicklinks.com**

# Houses and Homes

The type of home an animal has depends on how much protection it needs from enemies and the weather. Many animals do not have fixed homes, but wander in search of food. Some live in one area, called a territory, which they defend against intruders.

| Animal | Name of home |
|--------|--------------|
| Badger | Sett |
| Bat | Roost |
| Bear | Den |
| Beaver | Lodge |
| Fox | Den or earth |
| Hare | Form |
| Muskrat | House |
| Otter | Holt |
| Rabbit | Burrow or warren |
| Squirrel | Drey |

## Master builders

Beavers build their homes out of wood. With its strong teeth, a beaver can fell a tree half a metre thick in just 15 minutes.

*A beaver gnaws away at both sides of a tree trunk until the tree falls.*

The largest beaver dam ever built was 700m long and strong enough to bear the weight of a person riding across it on horseback. It was built on the Jefferson River, USA.

First, the beavers build a dam of logs and mud across a river to form a pond.

In the pond, they build a dome-shaped wooden lodge the size of a large tent.

They build a living area inside, which is above water level. To reach it, they dig underwater tunnels.

*Beaver lodges are made of sticks, logs, moss and grass.*

# Night nests

*Chimpanzee nest*

Orang-utans and chimpanzees build treetop nests to sleep in. They bend branches across to make a firm base and then weave smaller twigs into it. It only takes five minutes to build a nest.

# Mouse house

*Harvest mouse nest*

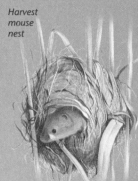

A harvest mouse builds its nest among tall grasses. With its teeth, it splits blades of grass into thin strips and weaves them into a framework. The blades are still joined to the stalks, so the nest is very secure.

# Prairie dog towns

Prairie dogs have the biggest burrows. They live in family groups called coteries. Areas where there are a lot of coteries are called prairie dog towns. The biggest prairie dog town ever found was in Texas, USA. About 160km wide and 400km long, the town was home to around 400 million prairie dogs.

*A prairie dog burrow usually has a nursery, toilet, grass-lined nesting chamber, and a listening post near the surface.*

*A Russian mole rat digs using its teeth.*

Russian mole rats are some of the fastest burrowers. They can shift 50 times their own weight in soil in around 20 minutes.

# Interior decorating

Badgers are very house-proud. They live in setts made up of chambers with connecting tunnels. They line their bedrooms with bracken, moss and grass. On dry mornings, they drag huge piles of bedding outside to air in the sun.

*Badgers close their eyes as they dig underground.*

INTERNET LINK

For a link to a website where you can explore a variety of animal homes, go to **www.usborne-quicklinks.com**

# Runners

Some animals are able to run very quickly to catch prey or escape from predators. Most fast-running animals run on their toes. Their ankles are half-way up their legs and their knees are close to their bodies.

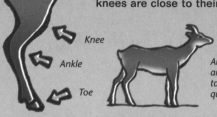

Knee

Ankle

Toe

*An antelope's legs are long and thin to help it run quickly.*

## Non-slip feet

An animal's hoofs stick into the ground and stop it from slipping. They do the same job as spikes on running shoes.

*Like shoes, hoofs prevent slipping.*

## Pronghorn puff

Pronghorns can run at a speed of 45kph for up to 15 minutes. To stop them from running out of breath or getting too tired, they have well-developed lungs and a heart twice as big as that of other animals of a similar size.

*A pronghorn can cover 6m in one stride.*

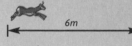

6m

Although they may look slow and clumsy, fully grown bears can run at a top speed of 40kph in short bursts. This is as fast as a galloping horse. Bears usually run quickly when chasing prey.

## The fastest facts

Cheetahs are the fastest animals on land. They can only run quickly for short distances though, and have a rest after running around 500m.

• Cheetahs can reach a top speed of 115kph, which is as fast as a family car.

• Cheetahs can reach 72kph from a standstill in just two seconds.

• Cheetahs have flexible backbones which allow them to take giant 7m leaps.

*A cheetah stretches its tail out for balance as it runs.*

### INTERNET LINK
For a link to website where you can watch a cheetah chase a gazelle, go to **www.usborne-quicklinks.com**

## Let's dance

Madagascan sifakas have legs much longer than their arms, so running on all fours along the ground is impossible. Instead, they do a running hop on their back legs. They bounce from one foot to the other, holding their arms high in the air.

*Sifakas spend most of their time in treetops and will only hop when they need to cross open ground.*

*A sifaka's strange run is called a "dance".*

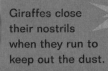

Giraffes close their nostrils when they run to keep out the dust.

*Giraffe with closed nostrils*

## Land waddlers

Both seals and sea lions are better at moving around in water than they are on land. On land or ice, seals can only drag themselves along on their bellies. Sea lions can turn their back flippers forward and waddle more easily than seals.

*A seal drags itself along.*

*A sea lion waddles.*

## Hopping hares

Hares not only run very quickly to escape predators, but also swerve and double back on their tracks to confuse the attacker. When they run, their long hind feet touch the ground in front of their forefeet, giving them a powerful push forward.

*Hare on the run*

| Fastest mammals | Top speed |
|---|---|
| Cheetah | 115kph |
| Pronghorn | 85kph |
| Wildebeest | 84kph |
| Mongolian gazelle | 80kph |
| Blackbuck | 78kph |
| Springbok | 77kph |
| Thomson's gazelle | 76kph |
| Brown hare | 72kph |
| Velk | 72kph |
| Race horse | 69kph |

# Climbers

Some animals find food and shelter high up in mountains and trees. To reach these places, they need to be good climbers.

## Helping hands

Asian tarsiers have suckers on their long fingers and toes to help them grip branches.

*Tarsier hand*

Like people, African pottos can move their thumbs across the palms of their hands. They also have a short first finger. This gives them a very strong grip.

*Pottos have specially adapted fingers.*

Sloths have claws that hook onto branches as they hang upside-down in trees.

*Sloths have hook-like claws.*

Adult spider monkeys sometimes stretch themselves between the branches of trees, making a bridge for their young to climb across.

*A mother spider monkey bridges the gap for her baby.*

## Spiny tails

Some types of porcupine have spines underneath their tails that help them to grip tree trunks. Some also have non-slip pads on the soles of their feet.

*Non-slip soles give porcupines extra grip.*

**INTERNET LINK**
For a link to a website about rainforest animal climbers, go to **www.usborne-quicklinks.com**

*A puma jumps out of a tree with its claws out to catch its unsuspecting prey.*

## Short cut

Most cats are good climbers but the puma has an even quicker way to get up and down trees. It is an excellent jumper. From a standstill, it can leap 7m – the height of four people – up into a tree. It can jump down to the ground from heights of up to 18m.

# Rock climbing

Ibexes can climb incredibly steep mountain slopes and jump from rock to rock, leaping over huge gaps. Their hoofs have narrow edges that dig into cracks in the rocks and slightly hollow soles that help them cling to rocky slopes.

*An ibex's sharp, hollow hoof can grip onto slippery and steep rocks.*

*When they sense danger, ibexes climb to the highest point they can reach.*

*Champion mountain climber*

Tschingle, a beagle dog, accompanied her owner up 53 of the most difficult mountains in the Alps, 11 of which had never been climbed before. In 1875, she climbed Mont Blanc, the highest mountain in the Alps, and was made a member of the exclusive Alpine Club.

## Quick climber

The fastest animal mountain climber is a type of mountain goat called a chamois. It lives in the Pyrenees and Alps in Europe and can climb 1,000m in only 15 minutes. A chamois could reach the top of Mount Everest in just over two hours.

*Chamois can leap up to 6m from one rock to another.*

## Leopard larder

A leopard drags its prey up into trees, where it is out of the reach of other animals that might want to steal it. When it has climbed high enough, it eats what it can and stores the rest among the branches.

| Highest living animals | Altitude |
|---|---|
| Marco Polo sheep | 7,000m |
| Pika | 6,100m |
| Snow leopard | 6,000m |
| Yak | 6,000m |
| Lesser mole rat | 4,000m |
| Mountain gorilla | 3,800m |

*Snow leopard*

# Animals in the Air

Some animals that live in trees have special flaps of skin that they use like wings. They don't fly, but glide from tree to tree as they search for food. Their front and back legs are joined by a flap of skin which acts as a parachute when they leap.

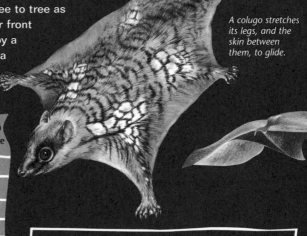

*A colugo stretches its legs, and the skin between them, to glide.*

| Longest gliders | Length of glide |
|---|---|
| Yellow-bellied glider | 115m |
| Giant flying squirrel | 100m |
| Greater glider | 100m |
| Colugo | 90m |
| Southern flying squirrel | 80m |
| Sugar glider | 50m |
| Northern flying squirrel | 50m |
| Feathertail glider | 20m |

### INTERNET LINK

For a link to a website where you can see amazing gliding animals, go to **www.usborne-quicklinks.com**

*Sugar gliders are very small – they are about the same length as a hamster.*

Squirrel monkeys sometimes leap straight up into the air from the treetops to catch insects. They can jump up to 2.5m from a standing start.

## Sweet gliders

A sugar glider gets its name from its sweet tooth. It likes sweet foods, such as tree sap and nectar. Sugar gliders are marsupials. This means that when a mother glides, she carries passengers – her babies are in a pouch on her stomach.

# True flight

The only mammals that can really fly are bats. Their wings are made of thin, leathery skin supported by long, bony fingers.

This is the bat's thumb.

Skin

Finger

Asian flying fox

Asian flying foxes are the world's largest bats. They have a 1.8m wingspan – about the same wingspan as a golden eagle.

## Hovering bats

Jamaican flower bats and tube-nosed fruit bats can hover. While hovering, they poke their long tongues into flowers to reach the nectar inside.

*A bat hovers by flapping its wings very quickly.*

## Flying fishermen

The American hare-lipped bat is an expert fisherman. It flies low over ponds and lakes, using echo location* to sense a fish just below the surface. It then swoops down and rakes the water with its large claws. Once the fish is caught, the bat carries it away to a branch or rock to eat.

*Hare-lipped bat on a successful fishing trip*

| Bat | Fastest speed | Similar speed to... |
| --- | --- | --- |
| Mexican free-tailed bat | 97kph | Car |
| Big brown bat | 64kph | Racehorse |
| Red bat | 60kph | Moped |
| Underwood's mastiff bat | 40kph | Water skier |
| Little brown bat | 19kph | In-line skater |

* See page 20

# Animals at Sea

Some animals, such as dolphins and whales, spend all their lives swimming in the sea.

*Dolphins and whales swim using flippers and a tail fin, like this one.*

Other sea animals, such as seals and walruses, live by the shore and spend some time on land.

*Seals and walruses have flipper-like back legs to help them move on land.*

**!** Orcas can swim six times faster than the fastest human swimmer, reaching a top speed of about 48kph. They use their strong tails as propellers to speed them through the water.

*Orca rocketing out of the sea*

## Sea unicorns

A narwhal only has two teeth. They grow straight forward from its top jaw. The male's left tooth is called a tusk. It grows in a spiral and can reach up to 2.5m long. Narwhals used to be killed for their tusks. Hunters would sell them as unicorn horns to be used in traditional medicines and to make ornaments.

*No one is quite sure what narwhals use their tusks for.*

## Ocean spray

Whales can't breathe underwater, so have to come up to the surface to take a breath. They suck in fresh air and blow out used air through a blowhole in the top of their heads. The warm air they blow out is full of moisture, which forms a spray of water droplets.

*A sperm whale's blowhole is on the left side of its head. This means that its spray shoots to the left.*

*A minke whale shoots a spray of water straight up into the air.*

*A right whale's blowhole is v-shaped and the spray shoots out in two streams.*

INTERNET LINK
For a link to a website where you can learn about whales, go to **www.usborne-quicklinks.com**

## Dolphin-napping

When a bottlenose dolphin goes to sleep, it closes only one eye so it can keep a look out for danger. It also shuts down only half of its brain. This is because it can't breathe automatically and has to decide when to come up to the surface for air. If it ever became fully unconscious, it would die. Every two hours, it swaps sides, resting the other side of its brain and closing the other eye. This pattern is called cat-napping.

## Seal tears

On land, seals often look like they are crying. This is because they produce tears to keep their eyes wet and clean. In the sea, the tears get washed away, but on land they trickle down the seals' cheeks.

*This seal's eyes are protected by thick, oily tears.*

Adult walruses, which can weigh over a tonne, use their tusks to drag themselves over the land. The Latin name for walrus, *Odobenus*, actually means "the one that walks with its teeth".

*This walrus is walking with its teeth.*

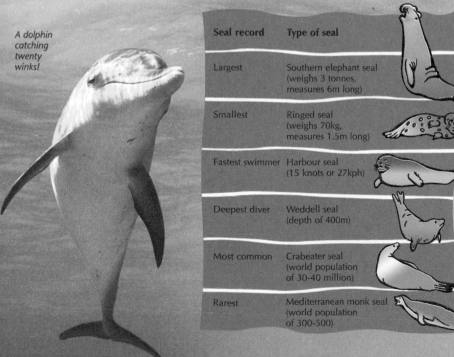

*A dolphin catching twenty winks!*

| Seal record | Type of seal |
| --- | --- |
| Largest | Southern elephant seal (weighs 3 tonnes, measures 6m long) |
| Smallest | Ringed seal (weighs 70kg, measures 1.5m long) |
| Fastest swimmer | Harbour seal (15 knots or 27kph) |
| Deepest diver | Weddell seal (depth of 400m) |
| Most common | Crabeater seal (world population of 30-40 million) |
| Rarest | Mediterranean monk seal (world population of 300-500) |

# Island Animals

Many types of animal can only be found on certain islands. They are different to mainland animals because they have developed in isolation, over millions of years.

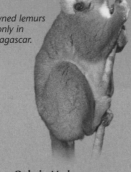

*Crowned lemurs live only in Madagascar.*

*The older an island is, the more time its animals have had to change – Madagascar is the oldest island shown, Galápagos is the youngest.*

— Australasia

Galápagos    Madagascar

| Only in Galápagos | Only in Australasia | Only in Madagascar |
|---|---|---|
| | | Fossas |
| | | Greater big-footed mice |
| | Dingoes | Lemurs |
| Fernandina rice rats | Echidnas | Malagasy civets |
| Galapágos fur seals | Kangaroos | Malagasy giant rats |
| Galapágos red bats | Koalas | Narrow-striped mongooses |
| Galapágos sea lions | Numbats | Sucker-footed bats |
| | Tasmanian devils | Tenrecs |
| Santa Fe rice rats | Wombats | White-tipped tufted-tailed rats |

## All mixed up

A fossa has a nose like a dog, teeth like a leopard, and whiskers like an otter. It is only the size of a fox, but is Madagascar's largest predator.

*Fossas jump from tree to tree, pouncing on lemurs, birds, frogs and lizards.*

**!** The Madagascan sportive lemur gets its name because, when it is attacked, it raises its fists like a boxer and punches its enemy.

INTERNET LINK
For a link to a website about unique Australian animals,
go to **www.usborne-quicklinks.com**

A Tasmanian devil sneezes when it wants to challenge another devil to a fight.

## Hairy seals

A Galápagos fur seal is very hairy. It has a thick coat made up of two layers of hair, one longer than the other. When a seal dives into the water, the long hairs fall over the small ones, trapping air between the two layers. The trapped air insulates the seal from the temperature of the water.

*A Galápagos fur seal dives into the water.*

*Air is trapped between the two layers of hair in its coat.*

*As the seal swims, air bubbles stream from its coat.*

## Expert diggers

Wombats live in burrows in Australia and Tasmania. Their bodies are specially adapted for digging. Even their pouch faces backwards so that the baby carried inside is not showered with earth as its mother digs.

*With its strong paws and claws, a wombat can dig as quickly as a person using a shovel.*

*While a mother wombat digs...*

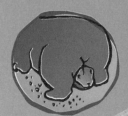

*...its baby looks out from its pouch, facing away from the flying dirt.*

## Tree hopping

In Australia and Papua New Guinea, some types of kangaroo live in trees. They move around by jumping between branches and can leap distances up to 15m. When they are on the ground, they can't jump so walk on all fours.

*This mother tree kangaroo will carry her baby in her pouch for as long as ten months.*

*A tree kangaroo grips onto a branch with its claws – because of these claws it can't hop along the ground.*

# Animals on Ice

Animals that live in very cold places have special ways of keeping warm, finding food and moving around on ice and snow.

## Black and white

*This polar bear's skin is actually black.*

A polar bear's coat acts like a thick, warm sweater. It is made of hollow hairs. Sunlight warms the air trapped in the hairs.

Beneath a polar bear's coat, its skin is black. Sunlight passes through the hairs and is then absorbed by the black skin. This also helps to keep the bear warm.

*Sunlight passes through its hairs and is absorbed by its black skin.*

Polar bears are strong swimmers but prefer to get around by using pieces of ice as rafts.

*Floating on a raft uses much less energy than swimming.*

## Snowshoes

Snowshoe rabbits get their name from their broad feet. These act like snowshoes and stop the rabbits sinking in the deep snow. Long hairs grow on the sides of their feet and between their toes. The hairs keep their feet warm and help them to grip the frozen ground. They can jump over 5m in one hop.

*Snowshoe rabbit*

### INTERNET LINK

For a link to a website where you can play a game about animals on ice, go to **www.usborne-quicklinks.com**

## Scraping snow

When snow covers the ground, caribou scrape holes in it to eat the lichen plants underneath. How the caribou know where to dig is a mystery. Perhaps they can smell the lichen under the snow.

*Caribou use their feet and antlers to dig up food.*

## Frozen fox food

In summer, Arctic foxes bury eggs and other food under the ground. When winter comes, they dig through the snow and ice to get to the deep-frozen food.

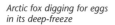

*Arctic fox digging for eggs in its deep-freeze*

Arctic foxes also get food by listening out for small animals under the snow. When they hear one, they jump up and down to break through the snow. Once the snow is broken, they can grab their prey.

| Mammals with coldest homes | Lives in temperatures as low as... |
|---|---|
| Arctic wolf | -75°C |
| Polar bear | -65°C |
| Musk ox | -60°C |
| Husky dog | -45°C |
| Caribou | -40°C |

*Musk ox*

## Cool patches

Vicuñas live high up in the snow-covered South American mountains. Despite the freezing temperatures, vicuñas can overheat because their coats are so warm. They have bare patches on their legs which they turn towards the wind to help them cool down.

*Vicuñas*

*Bath time for a macaque*

Japanese macaques keep warm by taking hot baths. During the winter, they spend most of their time sitting in hot, volcanic springs, often with the water right up to their necks.

*Arctic fox trying to break the ice to reach a group of lemmings hiding beneath*

# Desert Animals

Deserts are very dry places that have less than 25cm of rain a year. Hardly any plants grow there. Desert animals need ways to keep cool and to find enough to eat and drink in their hot, dry surroundings.

*You can see the blood vessels in this jack rabbit's ear.*

## Big ears

A jack rabbit uses its big ears to keep cool. The hot blood flowing in blood vessels near the surface is cooled by the air around them. To catch a slightly cooler breeze, the rabbit faces north.

## Air traps

A desert that is very hot by day can become very cold at night. Some desert animals have fur on their bodies that traps a layer of air. This layer insulates them from extreme heat or cold.

*Fur insulates the skin from heat during the day...*

*...and from cold at night.*

Desert wallabies and kangaroos use their own spit to keep themselves cool. When it is very hot, they pant and make a lot of saliva, which they lick all over themselves. As it evaporates, the saliva cools the animal down.

50

| Animals of the Sahara Desert | Animals of the Gobi Desert | Animals of the Arabian Desert | Animals of the Mojave Desert | Animals of the Great Victoria Desert |
|---|---|---|---|---|
| Addax | Mongolian gerbil | Arabian oryx | Jack rabbit | Kangaroo |
| Fennec fox | Gazelle | Striped hyena | Coyote | Wallaby |
| Jerboa | Bactrian camel (two humps) | Dromedary (camel with one hump) | Mojave ground squirrel | Dingo |
| Desert hedgehog | Gobi bear | Arabian gazelle | Bighorn sheep | Bilby |

# Underground cool

Some small desert animals spend their days underground to avoid the heat. Just 10cm below ground, the temperature can be up to 20° cooler than on the surface.

*A ground squirrel may burrow up to 1m below the ground.*

# Storage space

A camel can survive for nine days without water and 33 days without food. The secret is in its hump, which stores fat that can be used when there is no food. When it reaches water, a camel can drink 123 litres in ten minutes – about two-thirds of a bathtub full.

*A camel's hump can weigh up to 35kg – as much as a seven year old child.*

# Catching its breath

Jerboas save the moisture in their breath. They spend their days sleeping inside sealed burrows with their bushy tails over their mouths, to keep the moisture in.

*A jerboa catching its breath*

Jerboas even eat their own droppings for the moisture and vitamins they still contain.

*The addax is one of the world's rarest mammals.*

# No drinking

The addax, a rare antelope, never needs to drink. It gets all its moisture from the plants it eats. It is one of the very few large animals that is able to survive in the driest parts of the southern Sahara desert.

INTERNET LINK
For a link to a website about the animals of the Sahara desert, go to **www.usborne-quicklinks.com**

# Rainforest Animals

Rainforests grow near the Equator where it is always warm and rains nearly every day. The different levels of the rainforest are full of different types of animal.

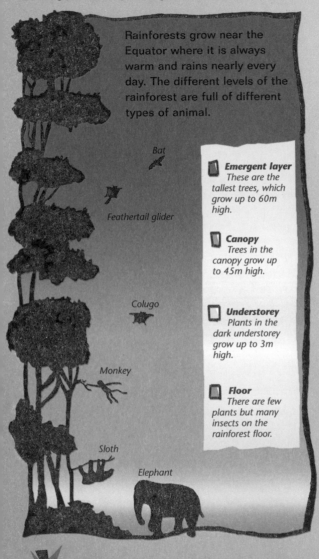

Bat

Feathertail glider

Colugo

Monkey

Sloth

Elephant

**Emergent layer**
These are the tallest trees, which grow up to 60m high.

**Canopy**
Trees in the canopy grow up to 45m high.

**Understorey**
Plants in the dark understorey grow up to 3m high.

**Floor**
There are few plants but many insects on the rainforest floor.

## Eating insects

Insect-eating animals, even big ones, find plenty to eat on the rainforest floor.

Aye-ayes have such good ears that they can hear insect grubs tunnelling in dead wood and fallen branches. They bite holes in the wood and use their long, skinny fingers to scrape out the grubs.

*An aye-aye listens for its next meal.*

Sun bears use their big paws to scoop ants out of ants' nests. Their tongues are long enough to poke into holes in logs, reaching insects hidden inside.

*A sun bear licks insects off its paws.*

During the rainy season, the Amazon River floods parts of the forest. Pink Amazon River dolphins can be seen swimming through the underwater trees.

## Bat tents

Some fruit bats make leaf "tents", which protect them from predators and the weather.

### INTERNET LINK

For a link to a website where you can go on a rainforest adventure, go to **www.usborne-quicklinks.com**

A fruit bat chews leaves at the base near the stem.

The leaves collapse to form a shelter.

| Animals of the Asian rainforests | Animals of the South American rainforests | Animals of the African rainforests |
| --- | --- | --- |
| Bengal tiger | Giant anteater | Bushbaby |
| Common palm civet | Marmoset | Chimpanzee |
| Orang-utan | Panther | Gorilla |
| Silvery gibbon | Squirrel monkey | Hippopotamus |
| Sumatran rhinoceros | Tapir | Hyrax |

## Water pigs

Capybaras look like a cross between a beaver and a pig. Their scientific name, *Hydrochoerus*, means "water pig". They live along ponds and rivers in rainforests and have partially webbed feet. When threatened, they will often jump in the water and hide.

Capybaras swim well but walk clumsily because of their webbed feet.

Capybaras keep cool in the water.

## Killer otters

Giant otters are among the most successful predators in the Brazilian rainforest and have even been known to kill anacondas. People are their only predators.

## Wake up call

Howler monkeys howl at regular times – their loud calls "wake up" the rainforest in the morning and "put it to bed" at night. Sometimes they howl just before it rains, like a sort of weather forecast.

Howler monkeys are the loudest rainforest animals.

Howler monkeys sometimes tease jaguars – but from a safe distance up in the trees. They throw sticks at the jaguar below. The jaguar, meanwhile, waits for an unfortunate howler to slip and fall.

# Grassland Animals

Grasslands are open and windy areas of land where grasses and low bushes grow. For most of the year, grasslands are very dry. Lots of different plant eaters live on grasslands and are hunted by meat eaters.

| Browsers (eat leaves) | Grazers (eat grass) | Predators (eat meat) |
| --- | --- | --- |
| Giraffes | Zebras | Lions |
| Elephants | Wildebeest | Cheetahs |
| Black rhinoceroses | White rhinoceroses | Leopards |
| Kudus | Hippopotamuses | Hunting dogs |
| Gerenuks | Bison | Hyenas |
| | Warthogs | Servals |

*This kudu is running for its life.*

*This lion is about to catch its next meal.*

## Working together

Hunting dogs, hyenas and lions usually chase animals that are larger and faster than them. To catch their prey, they work together in pairs or small groups. Once the animal is caught, the group shares the food.

*Hunting dogs on the look-out for prey*

## In and out

A warthog always enters its burrow backwards, so it can fight off enemies with its tusks while backing in. In the mornings, it bursts out of its burrow at top speed to get a running start on any enemies that may be watching.

*A warthog never turns its back on an enemy.*

Bat-eared foxes have such excellent hearing that they can even hear termites moving underground. They then dig up the termites and eat them.

*This fox's ears pick up the tiniest sounds.*

# Grassland groups

Many animals roam the grassland in groups.
The groups are organized in different ways:

**Lion prides** are led by a few males whose job is to protect the females. Females hunt and take care of the cubs.

**Baboon troops** are led by an older male. He keeps everyone together and defends his troop if it is attacked.

*Leader of a baboon troop*

*Females and cubs of a lion pride*

*Wildebeest*

**Wildebeest herds** are always on the move. They have no leader and members come and go as they please.

**Gerenuks** are the only hoofed animals that can stand on their hind legs.

*A gerenuk balances on its hind legs to reach up for a snack.*

### INTERNET LINK
For a link to a website where you can become a grassland wildlife photographer, go to **www.usborne-quicklinks.com**

## Shelter below

There are not many places to hide or shelter from the weather on grasslands, so many small animals live underground. Some come up to the surface to find food but others spend all their lives underground.

- Mole rats live under the African grasslands.

- Black-bellied hamsters live under the Asian grasslands.

- Gophers live under the prairies – the North American grasslands.

- Maras live under the pampas – the South American grasslands.

# Animals in Danger

When a type of animal dies out, is it said to be extinct. If it is likely to die out unless we take action, it is said to be threatened or endangered.

In parts of Africa, people are trying to save rare rhinos by sawing off their horns so that hunters will leave them alone. Rhinos are hunted so that their horns can be used in traditional medicines.

*Rhino with two sawn-off horns*

## Growing number

In the 1970s, there were only 200 golden lion tamarins in the wild. The places where they lived were being damaged, and they were being hunted and captured for the pet trade, zoos and medical research. Now they live in protected parts of the rainforest and it is illegal to hunt them. By 2001, their number had grown to 1,000.

*Golden lion tamarin*

## Small world

*A mountain gorilla in its rainforest home*

Mountain gorillas must be very attached to their natural habitat, as none have ever survived in captivity. There are only around 600 mountain gorillas left in the world and they all live in an area of African rainforest measuring just 740km$^2$.

| Recently extinct animals | Last seen... |
| --- | --- |
| Pyrean ibex | 2000 |
| Javan tiger | 1980 |
| Barbary lion | 1960 |
| Japanese sea lion | 1951 |
| Tasmanian tiger-wolf | 1936 |
| Martinique muskrat | 1902 |
| Quagga | 1883 |

| Most endangered mammals | Found in... | Population in wild (2001) |
|---|---|---|
| 1 Baiji dolphin | China | Fewer than 40 |
| 2 Seychelles sheath-tailed bat | Seychelles | Fewer than 50 |
| 3 Javan rhinoceros | Indonesia; Vietnam | Fewer than 60 |
| 4 Northern hairy-nosed wombat | Australia | 60 |
| 5 Hisipid hare | India; Nepal | 110 |
| 6 Black-footed ferret | North America | Fewer than 200 |
| 7 Tonkin snub-nosed monkey | Vietnam | 200 |
| 8 Kouprey | Cambodia | Fewer than 250 |
| 9 Yellow-tailed woolly monkey | Peru | Fewer than 250 |
| 10 Visayan spotted deer | Philippines | Fewer than 500 |

## Ferret FM

When the black-footed ferret population was down to just 18, scientists began to breed them in captivity. Today, when young ferrets are released into the wild, they are fitted with radio collars so that people can keep track of them.

*Signals transmitted from the radio collar are picked up by a receiver.*

## Dangerous waters

Speedboats are the greatest threat to rare manatees, which swim slowly, near the surface of the water. In one year, 218 manatees in the USA were killed and many more were injured when hit by boats.

INTERNET LINK

For a link to a website where you can visit an endangered animal hotel, go to **www.usborne-quicklinks.com**

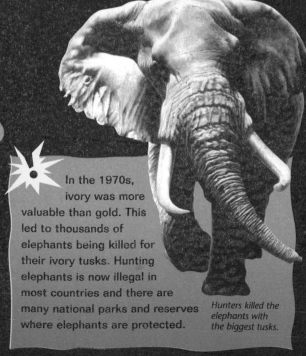

In the 1970s, ivory was more valuable than gold. This led to thousands of elephants being killed for their ivory tusks. Hunting elephants is now illegal in most countries and there are many national parks and reserves where elephants are protected.

*Hunters killed the elephants with the biggest tusks.*

# Biome Map

A biome is a large area with one main type of climate and one main type of vegetation. This map shows the seven principal biomes and some of the animals found in them.

Brown bear

Fox

ASIA

EUROPE

AFRICA

Ibex

African elephant

AUSTRALASIA

Camel

Sperm whale

**Key**
- Poles and tundra
- Deserts
- Grasslands
- Mountains
- Coniferous forests
- Deciduous forests
- Rainforests

Kangaroo

Beaver

Polar bear

NORTH AMERICA

Raccoon

Sloth

Manatee

SOUTH AMERICA

Dolphin

**INTERNET LINK**

For a link to a website where you can explore different biomes, go to **www.usborne-quicklinks.com**

Leopard seal

ANTARCTICA

59

# Glossary

**Aestivation** A deep sleep or time of inactivity to save energy and keep cool during very hot and dry weather.

**Biome** A large area with one main type of climate and one main type of vegetation.

**Breeding** When a male and female animal join together to produce young.

**Browsers** Animals that eat leaves.

**Camouflage** Special colourings or markings that help animals to disguise themselves.

**Captivity** Being within a small space.

**Coniferous forests** Forests made up of narrow-leaved, evergreen trees.

**Deciduous forests** Forests made up of trees that lose their leaves before winter.

**Desert** An area of land where there is very little rain and few plants.

**Digestion** When food is broken down and its nutrients absorbed inside an animal's body.

**Echo location** Using sound waves to work out where objects are.

**Endangered** A species of animal that is at risk of dying out.

**Equator** An imaginary line drawn around the middle of the Earth an equal distance from the North and South Pole.

**Extinct** Animals that no longer exist. They become officially extinct if there have been no certain records of them for 50 years.

**Grasslands** Open and windy areas of land where grasses and low bushes grow.

**Gravity** A force that pulls objects towards the Earth's core.

**Grazers** Animals that eat grass.

**Habitat** The natural surroundings in which an animal or plant lives.

**Herd** A group of animals that live and feed together.

**Hibernation** A deep sleep or time of inactivity to save energy during the cold winter months.

**Hoof** Horny part of an animal's foot.

**Insectivores** Animals that mainly eat insects.

**Keratin** The substance that makes up fingernails and hair.

**Krill** Small, shrimp-like ocean creatures.

**Life cycle** The series of changes an animal goes through during its life.

**Marsupials** Mammals with pouches.

**Mammals** A group of warm-blooded animals that have hair and feed their young on milk from their bodies.

**Maturity** Being fully grown physically.

**Migration** Travelling to a different place in order to live there for a season.

**Nocturnal** An animal that is most active at night.

**Predators** Animals that hunt and eat other animals.

**Prey** An animal that is hunted for food by other animals.

**Rainforests** Dense, warm forests that have at least 2.5m of rainfall each year.

**Scavengers** Animals that feed on dead animals that they have not killed themselves.

**Teat** A lobe of tissue on a female mammal's body through which milk is passed.

**Territory** An area which an animal "owns" and defends against intruders.

**Tundra** A large area of land where the ground is frozen in winter.

**Warm-blooded** Animals that can control their own body temperature so it always stays the same, whatever the temperature of their surroundings.

# Using the Internet

## Internet links

Most of the websites described in this book can be accessed with a standard home computer and an Internet browser (the software that enables you to display information from the Internet). We recommend:

• A PC with Microsoft® Windows® 98 or later version, or a Macintosh computer with System 9.0 or later, and 64Mb RAM
• A browser such as Microsoft® Internet Explorer 5, or Netscape® 6, or later versions
• Connection to the Internet via a modem (preferably 56Kbps) or a faster digital or cable line
• An account with an Internet Service Provider (ISP)
• A sound card to hear sound files

## Extras

Some websites need additional free programs, called plug-ins, to play sounds, or to show videos, animations or 3-D images. If you go to a site and you do not have the necessary plug-in, a message saying so will come up on the screen. There is usually a button on the site that you can click on to download the plug-in. Alternatively, go to www.usborne-quicklinks.com and click on "Net Help". There you can find links to download plug-ins. Here is a list of plug-ins you might need:

**RealOne Player®** – lets you play videos and hear sound files
**QuickTime** – lets you view video clips
**Shockwave®** – lets you play animations and interactive programs
**Flash™** – lets you play animations

## Help

For general help and advice on using the Internet, go to **Usborne Quicklinks** at **www.usborne-quicklinks.com** and click on **Net Help**. To find out more about how to use your web browser, click on **Help** at the top of the browser, and then choose Contents and Index. You'll find a huge searchable dictionary containing tips on how to find your way around the Internet.

## Internet safety

Remember to follow the Internet safety guidelines at the front of this book. For more safety information, go to **Usborne Quicklinks** and click on **Net Help**.

## Computer viruses

A computer virus is a program that can seriously damage your computer. A virus can get into your computer when you download programs from the Internet, or in an attachment (an extra file) that arrives with an email. We strongly recommend that you buy anti-virus software to protect your computer, and that you update the software regularly.

> **INTERNET LINK**
> For a link to a website where you can find out more about computer viruses, go to **www.usborne-quicklinks.com** and click on **Net Help**.

# Index

# Acknowledgements

Every effort has been made to trace the copyright holders of the material in this book. If any rights have been omitted, the publishers offer to rectify this in any subsequent editions following notification. The publishers are grateful to the following organizations and individuals for their permission to reproduce material (t=top, m=middle, b=bottom, l=left, r=right):

AnimalsAnimals: **15b** Wegner, Jorg & Petra/AnimalsAnimals/Earth Scenes; **35t** Mendez, Raymond/AnimalsAnimals/Earth Scenes
Corbis: **1** Nigel J. Dennis, Gallo Images/CORBIS; **2-3** George D. Lepp/CORBIS; **6b** John Conrad/CORBIS; **8b** Gallo Images/CORBIS; **11br** Bettmann/CORBIS; **17b** Tom Brakefield/CORBIS; **20r** James L. Amos/CORBIS; **22bl** Anthony Bannister, Gallo Images/CORBIS; **23tm** Theo Allofs/CORBIS; **24b** Raymond Gehman/CORBIS; **26bm** Paul A. Souders/CORBIS, **mr** Kennan Ward/CORBIS; **28tm** Gunter Marx Photography/CORBIS; **33b** Owen Franken/CORBIS; **36b** Rose Hartman/CORBIS; **41tr** Giry Daniel/CORBIS SYGMA; **46b** Chris Hellier/CORBIS; **51br** Steve Kaufman/CORBIS; **53b** Kevin Schafer/CORBIS; **54m** Gallo Images/CORBIS; **56tr** Terry Whittaker, Frank Lane Picture Agency/CORBIS
Digital Vision: **8ml**; **9tr, ml**; **13mr**; **16bl**; **18b**; **27b, tl**; **30tr**; **34m, mr, bl**; **39tr**; **45bl**; **46tr**; **50t**; **55tl, tm**
Husar: **48t** Lisa and Mike Husar/TeamHusar.com
Getty Images: **24mr** Anup Shah/Getty Images; **31br** Getty Images/PhotoDisc
Ken Catania: **21b** Ken Catania, Vanderbilt University, Nashville, Tennessee
Nature Picture Library: **17ml** Jeff Foott/Nature Picture Library
Natural History Photographic Agency: **39tm** Andy Rouse/NHPA
Science Photo Library: **43m** Merlin Tuttle/Science Photo Library

**Additional illustrators** Ian Jackson, Rachel Lockwood, Malcolm McGregor, Chris Shields, David Wright

**Additional designer** Michael Hill

Material in this book is based on *The Usborne Book of Animal Facts* by Anita Ganeri, © Usborne Publishing, 1988.